Chapter 1

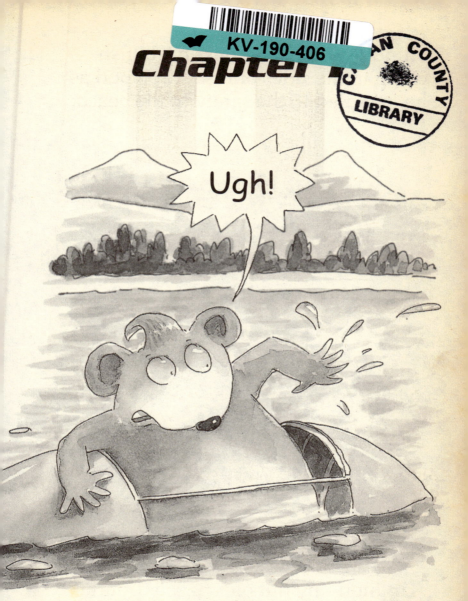

Something slimy brushed against
Onlee One's paw.

Hundreds of putrid, green jellyfish clung to the sides of his escape pod as he paddled to the safety of the beach.

A million tiny bubbles fizzed around him. The jellyfish were eating away the metal skin of the escape pod!

Onlee One tried to pick one off but it stung him.

"Ow!" he squealed.

After everything I've been through, I'm going to end up being eaten alive by jellyfish!

Onlee One closed his eyes and waited
for the end.

Chapter 2

Meanwhile, across the vast distance of space, Dark Claw paced the control room of Dark Moon.

Once again, Onlee One had escaped his clutches and sent him flying into a rage.

"He must be destroyed!" Dark Claw roared.

Onlee One will meet a slow and painful end, I will make sure of it! But first ... I must complete my master plan.

With his army of Robo Kats and attack ships, Dark Claw intended to rid the universe of the entire population on Planet Muss.

Dark Claw turned to the Robo Kat captain.

"We must move quickly. We need more attack ships and we need them now! We cannot lose the element of surprise."

The captain's thin, metallic voice replied.

Yes Dark Claw. Your will is our command!"

Chapter 3

Meanwhile, something massive
rumbled behind Onlee One's pod.
He turned and stared in horror.

A giant, scaly, purple sea-serpent
loomed above him. Its fierce jaws
were crammed with hundreds of tiny,
needle-sharp teeth.

The serpent lunged at Onlee One. "Oh no! I'm going to be snake meat!" he screamed, as the monster crashed down into the water. Onlee One smelled its evil breath and felt the escape pod rise on a tidal wave.

Onlee One opened one eye. He was still alive. The sea monster had simply scooped up a mouthful of jellyfish and eaten them. Now it lunged towards him again, and again.

Each time the monster moved, the waves pushed Onlee One closer to the beach, but his escape pod was sinking.

Suddenly, the pod hit a sand bank. As Onlee One leapt out and into the water, the pod sank below the surface.

The sand was soft underfoot, making it difficult to wade through the water.

The jellyfish stung him and his lungs were ready to burst, but he drove himself on through the surf until, at last, he collapsed on the warm dry sand.

"I did it!" Onlee One gasped.

Chapter 4

Onlee One found his spaceship on
the beach. It had belonged to the
Pi-rats who were going to sell him to
Dark Claw. The autopilot had landed
it safely. It seemed to be okay.

Onlee One had just escaped from the
prison planet, Pen. He hadn't eaten
proper food for weeks. He set off to try
and find some fresh fruit.

Ten minutes later, he came across two large, deeply carved stones that stood like gateposts in the sand.

The stones marked the entrance to a path that led deep into the jungle.

Onlee One's whiskers twitched. Maybe he wasn't alone on this planet, after all?

He followed the path until it opened out into a mossy glade. A tree stood in the middle. It shimmered in a multitude of colours. Warily, Onlee One crossed the glade for a closer look.

"Ribbons!" he whispered in surprise. The tree was covered in them! "I am definitely not alone!" he thought.

Two more stone gateposts stood at the entrance to a strange building made from huge rocks. The roof was covered in grass.

Onlee One crept inside.

A dark corridor led him to a circular room, like a chapel. Daylight filtered down from the roof. A Kat's paw was carved above the altar.

He'd seen the sign before, on planet Kat. It was something to do with The *Guiding Paw*, the religion of the Kats.

As he turned to go, his heart thumped to a stop.

Twelve, tall creatures in long, red, hooded robes, watched him from the shadows. Their yellow eyes glowed beneath their hoods. He couldn't see their faces, but he knew they were Kats.

"Hi!" he said, cheerfully. "Nice place you've got here." If he was nice to them, maybe they wouldn't sacrifice him … just yet!

Chapter 5

The Kats led Onlee One through the jungle. Ribbons tied to trees seemed to mark out their route. Nobody spoke. Then suddenly, the jungle stopped and Onlee One gasped at what he saw.

A cliff rose up in front of them.
A Kat town, had been carved out of
the rock, but there were Muss-holes
all over the place.

Onlee One made his way up a sweeping staircase. At the top, a tall white Kat in a vivid red robe waited for him. Kats and Muss watched his progress.

The white Kat spoke softly.

Welcome to Libera. Have no fear. Here, Kat and Muss live together in peace.

She said her name was Spyra and she was the chosen leader. She told Onlee One of the terrible war between Kats and Muss that had destroyed the beautiful planet of Felicity.

Many of the Kats and Muss were ashamed of what the war had done. They vowed to come to Libera, and learn to live together.

Food and drink was brought for Onlee One, and then he told Spyra his story.

When he mentioned Dark Claw, Spyra's face clouded over. She looked to the sky and sighed.

The Dark Claw you speak of is my son!

Onlee One was shocked. It was hard to
believe that this beautiful, gentle Kat
could be the mother of such an evil
menace as Dark Claw.

Onlee One held her gaze.

If Dark Claw is
your son, then you
once knew my father,
Pale One.

Her eyes narrowed as she examined his features. Then she nodded, seeing the likeness to his father in his face.

There was a movement behind her.
An older Muss, who had been standing
in the shadows came to her side.

"I am Pale One!" he said.

Chapter 6

"It was Brandling that told me you and your Mother had died, sighed Pale One. "After that, there was nothing left for me to do on Muss."

Onlee One had told his story. Now it was his father's turn.

"When Dark Claw was a kitten," Pale One explained, "he caught a bad cold from me and became so ill that he was unable to walk and grew up needing a wheelchair."

"I thought you were dead, " he told Onlee One. "So I returned to help look after Dark Claw. After all, it was my fault that he had become so ill."

Pale One looked sad. The memories came flooding back to him. "Dark Claw was always angry. We thought it was because he couldn't walk. But perhaps he was just plain bad.

He was very clever. He made his own Robo-suit that allowed him to walk. Then, when his father died in a tragic accident, Dark Claw disappeared. Spyra came here and I came with her."

Onlee One listened to his father intently. He felt he had known him all his life.

Will you come and help us fight Dark Claw, Father?

Pale One smiled. "I never thought I'd hear myself called Father…" He held out his arms and hugged Onlee One.

"…But I have vowed to spend my life working for peace," Pale One said to his son.

This is your fight, Son. It's up to you now.

Chapter 7

Onlee One's spaceship sped across the Universe. He was bound for Planet Pen on a mission to rescue his friends, Hammee and Chin Chee .

A few kind Muss on Libera had helped him clean up the ship and load it with provisions.

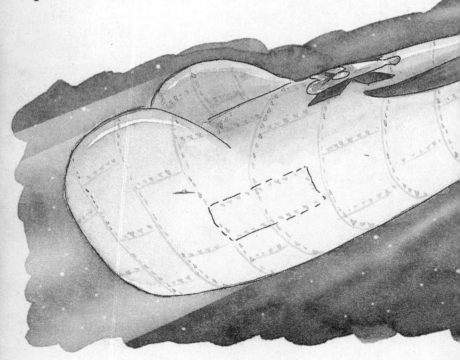

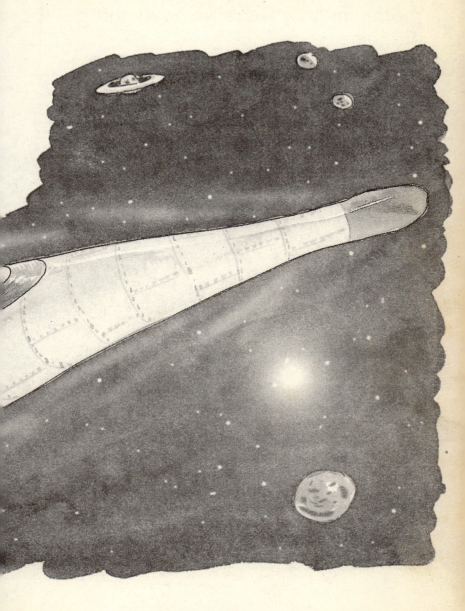

Onlee One looked out of the control room window. There was something out there.

Dark Moon!

It was surrounded by a huge fleet of
Robo Kat ships… hundreds of them!
Onlee One filmed them with a vid-cam.

Then he pointed the vid-cam at the
Nosar screen and spoke aloud for the
camera.

None of these ships
show up on the screen. Dark
Claw has found a way to be
invisible to Nosar!

He quickly altered course before he was spotted and attacked. It wasn't long before Pen came into sight.

Brandling had given a gold disk to Ratuschka, the leader of the Pi-rats. It was a passport that allowed anyone to land on Pen without trouble. Onlee One slipped it into a disk drive on the control desk.

Onlee One flew right down to the planet's surface, and across to where he knew his friends Hammee and Chin Chee would be.

He hovered by the treadmills. His voice boomed over the loudspeakers.

When his two old friends saw Onlee One's ship, smiles broke out on their faces and they ran towards it.

Onlee One hardly recognised Hammee – he'd lost so much weight!

Hammee and Chin Chee climbed on board and rushed to the control room where they were reunited with their old friend.

With tears in his eyes, Hammee hugged Onlee One till he could hardly breathe. Then he asked, "I don't suppose there's anything to eat?!"

Chapter 8

"Pooh! Disgusting!" said Hammee. The three friends were in a sewer underneath the President's palace.

The gold disk had allowed the trio to land close to the palace. The sewers were the only way in.

Onlee One climbed a ladder up to a Muss-hole cover. Gently, he raised it just a crack, and peered into a courtyard.

They climbed out of the hole, quietly replaced the lid, and ran to the shadows. Onlee One had met Top Muss before. With his incredible sense of smell, he now detected the faintest scent of the leader.

The three friends crept through corridors and tiptoed down passages.

"He's behind that door," whispered Onlee One. "And so is Brandling!"

"What about the guards?" hissed Chin Chee.

Onlee One took out Brandling's gold disk passport. "Let's try this."

Boldly, they walked toward the guards. Onlee One waved the disk at them.

"We've important news for Chancellor Brandling," he announced.

The guards looked unsure. But Onlee One *was* carrying Brandling's passport, so they opened the doors and let them in. The three young Muss rushed into the President's office.

Chapter 9

Brandling stood next to the President. They were looking at some papers. Brandling's jaw dropped when she saw who had just burst into the room.

Onlee One spoke. "Your honour, our planet is in great danger. Dark Claw is building a huge army that cannot be detected by Nosar." Onlee One held up the vid-cam.

I have proof.

Brandling laughed. "What nonsense! Who ever heard of such a thing?"

Guards! Arrest these fools!

Onlee One held up the gold disk that Brandling had given to the Pi-rats.

I also have proof of Chancellor Brandling's treachery!

Top Muss held up a paw to stop the guards. He spoke with great authority. "I think we should see the evidence before we make up our minds."

Brandling smiled nervously. "Of course, your honour!"

They watched the video in silence.
When it had finished, Top Muss was
ashen-faced. He stayed silent for a
moment, deep in thought, then he
spoke.

Well, what do
you have to say
for yourself,
Brandling?!

But Brandling had gone! She had
slipped out of a side door while they
were watching the video.

Onlee One explained to Top Muss how Brandling had imprisoned him, Hammee and Chin Chee and was working in league with Dark Claw.

"I have often doubted Brandling's loyalty," said Top Muss. "Never have the Muss faced such a fearful enemy as Dark Claw. And thanks to Brandling's treachery he has grown even more powerful."

Brandling laughed. "What nonsense!
Who ever heard of such a thing?"

Onlee One held up the gold disk that
Brandling had given to the Pi-rats.

Top Muss held up a paw to stop the guards. He spoke with great authority. "I think we should see the evidence before we make up our minds."

Brandling smiled nervously. "Of course, your honour!"

Top Muss put an arm on Onlee One's shoulder. "You have done well, young Onlee One. Let us hope we are not too late!"

Top Muss called out to the guards.

Search the palace. Arrest Brandling. She must not escape!

Chapter 9

Meanwhile, Dark Claw had received news of Onlee One's escape. He gave orders to his Robo Kat fleet.

"We must not lose the element of surprise." He told his Robo Army. "The invasion of Planet Muss is about to begin!"

Dark Claw almost purred with satisfaction, as he watched his vast fleet of spaceships prepare for battle stations.

Have you seen the Dark Claw Website?

www.dark-claw.co.uk

Shoo Rayner designed and built the Dark Claw Website
himself, while he was writing the Dark Claw stories.
It is packed full of games and background stories about the
worlds of Onlee One, his friends and his enemies!

Why is Dark Claw so angry?
Why does he want to destroy the Muss?

 Where in the Universe is the planet Muss?
What is Litterbox? What is Kimono?

What is it like at the Tan Monastery School?
Why do the beds squeak?

All this and more. If you're a Dark Claw fan, you'll love the
Dark Claw website. It's all part of the story!

If you enjoyed this book you'll want to read the other books in the Dark Claw Saga.

Tunnel Mazers
0 340 81754 2
The one with the very
smelly cheese!

Road Rage
0 340 81755 0
The one with the cool
racing machines!

Rat Trap
0 340 81756 9
The one with invisible
space ships!

Breakout!
0 340 81757 7
The one with nowhere
left to go!

The Guiding Paw
0 340 81758 5
The one with the Muss-
eating jellyfish!

The Black Hole
0 340 81759 3
The one with the end
of the story!

**Find out more about Shoo Rayner and his other
fantastic books at www.shoo-rayner.co.uk**

If you enjoyed this book you'll love these other books by Shoo Rayner and Hodder Children's Books

The Rex Files
(Seriously weird!)

0 340 71432 8 The Life-Snatcher
0 340 71466 2 The Phantom Bantam
0 340 71467 0 The Bermuda Triangle
0 340 71468 9 The Shredder
0 340 71469 7 The Frightened Forest
0 340 71470 0 The Baa-Baa Club

Or what about the wonderful
Ginger Ninja?

0 340 61955 4 The Ginger Ninja
0 340 61956 2 The Return of Tiddles
0 340 61957 0 The Dance of the Apple Dumplings
0 340 61958 9 St Felix for the Cup
0 340 69379 7 World Cup Winners
0 340 69380 0 Three's a Crowd

And don't forget SUPERDAD!
(He's a bit soft really!)

0 7500 2694 4 Superdad
0 7500 2706 1 Superdad the SuperHero

Phone 012345 400414 and have a credit card ready

Please allow the following for postage and packing:
UK & BFPO – £1.00 for the first book, 50p for the second book, and 30p for
each additional book ordered up to a maximum charge of £3.00.
OVERSEAS & EIRE – £2.00 for the first book, £1.00 for the second book,
and 50p for each additional book.